Contents

KT-467-761

Con

Josh

CHAPTER 1

Boys in Space

Best friends Con and Josh have spent the morning in Josh's room, reading a book about spaceships.

Con "How good would it be if we were astronauts?"

Josh "Yes, being able to fly into space would be really great!"

Con "We would be sort of like Darth Vader."

Josh "We would rule all of outer space."

Con "And when aliens attacked—we would just shoot them."

Josh "I wonder where you get a spaceship?"

Con "Not sure, but I bet you don't buy them from a shop."

Josh "Yes, if you could, everyone would be flying around in them. Nobody would drive a car."

Con "That would be so cool. Then all the roads could be turned into skateboard ramps."

Josh "Where would people park their spaceships?"

Con "They would have to park them on top of their houses! They would have to build special spaceship garages on their roofs."

CHAPTER 2

Alien Invasion!

Con and Josh wander outside and stand under their tree house.

Con "I think that we could build our own spaceship."

Josh (pointing) "Yes, and when we do, we can park it on top of our tree house."

Con "We'll be able to launch it from there as well."

Josh "Straight into the stratosphere!"

Con "Our spaceship will be so good that we will probably be asked to join the army and protect the world from aliens."

Josh "Have you ever seen any aliens?"

Con "Yes, I saw some once, in this movie called 'Alien Attack'."

Josh "How scary would the world be
if aliens ran it?"

Con "Really scary, especially if they
were like the ones that I saw in the
movie."

Josh "They would probably have
green snot running down their face."

Con "And only one eye in the middle
of their head."

Josh "But the good thing is that they would only eat girls."

Con "Aliens wouldn't even think about eating boys—boys are *far* too tough to eat."

Josh "Wonder what you need to build a spaceship?"

Con "Don't know. Bits and pieces of everything, I suppose."

Josh (smiling) "And I think most of those are in my father's garage. He's got heaps of great bits and pieces."

Con "Do you think that he will mind us using all his stuff?"

Josh "Naaah—not if we tell him that we're going to save the world from aliens."

Con "Might be better not to tell him until after we've built the spaceship."

CHAPTER 3

The *Snot Attack*

The boys soon get busy in the garage
collecting boxes, nails and tins. When
they put them all together, they have
something that looks like—well, a bit
like a spaceship.

Josh "So, what do you think?"

Con "Well, it looks like something—
but it's not much like the spaceship
that I saw in 'Alien Attack'."

Josh "Yes, but still, if any alien sees
us in this, they'll take off and head
straight back to Alien Land."

Con "Only if we don't blow them to
pieces first."

Josh "What will we call our spaceship?"

Con "Well, if aliens have green snot running down their faces and we're going to be destroying aliens, then we should call our spaceship 'Snot Attack'."

Josh "Great name! Hey, I want to be captain."

Con "No way! You always want to be captain."

Josh "Well, OK. Maybe this time we could be joint captains."

Con "Cool. You can be Captain Snot of the *Snot Attack* spaceship and I could be Captain Green."

Josh (laughing) "That means we'll be Captains Green and Snot of the spaceship *Snot Attack*. Excellent!"

Con and Josh find a can of spray paint in the garage and paint a bright green sign that says "Snot Attack" on the side of the spaceship.

Josh "Wow, we're nearly ready to go into orbit."

Con "All we need to do now is set up our control base."

Josh "Well, we can use the old television from the garage as our monitor."

Con "And when any aliens appear on the screen, that's when we'll blast into action."

Josh "Great, now all we need to do is stock our spaceship with supplies before we blast-off."

Con "Yes, we need lots of food."

Josh "Mum made some great chocolate cake yesterday, and I know where she hid the cake tin."

Con "All the best alien fighters eat chocolate cake."

Josh "We could grab some oranges, too, and use them as bombs."

Con "I think if you hit an alien with an orange, the juice would get all mixed up with their green snot and they would probably sneeze and blow their heads off."

CHAPTER 4

Time for Blast-off!

Con and Josh load their spaceship with all the supplies.

Josh "I think we're ready for the alien attack."

Con "So, how are we going to launch the spaceship?"

Josh (scratching his head) "Hmmm, I've got a great idea."

Con "Yes, what?"

Josh "Well, we can get a plank out of the garage and rest it on that big barrel over there."

Con "Cool, then we can put the spaceship on one end and drop something heavy on the other end."

Josh "We'll go straight into orbit if we do that!"

Con "But how are we going to drop something on the end of the plank if we're both in the spaceship?"

Josh "Well, maybe one of us has to be in the spaceship when we launch it. Then they come back and pick up the other one."

Con "Good thinking, Captain Snot."

Josh "I think that I should get to captain the spaceship on its first flight!"

Con "Why you?"

Josh "Because you always go first."

Con "No, I don't. You do."

Josh "Well, this looks like a 'stone, paper, scissors' thing."

Con "OK. Are you ready? One, two, three ..."

Josh "Stone!"

Con "Paper!"

Josh "Paper covers stone. Looks like you win."

Con "Right, I get to fly, and you get to control the blast-off."

The boys take a plank from the
garage and rest it over the barrel.
They load the spaceship onto one end
of the plank.

CHAPTER 5

Out of Control!

The boys sit staring at the monitor.

Josh "Look! A message from space control—the aliens are coming!"

Con "We need to blast-off. We've got to hurry before the aliens destroy the Earth!"

Both boys run and get dressed for the space mission ... crash helmets, gloves and kneepads. Josh climbs to the top of the garage and Con gets into the spaceship.

Josh "Are you ready, Captain Green?"
Con "Yes, I'm ready, Captain Snot."

Josh "Begin countdown."

Con "Ten, nine, eight, seven, six, five, four, three, two, one—blast-off!"

Josh jumps from the garage roof, landing on the end of the plank without the spaceship. Both Con and the spaceship are catapulted into the air.

Con *"Wheeeeee!"*

The spaceship's descent is even
faster than its blast-off. It goes over
the fence into Mr. Grumbleguts's
garden next door. Mr. Grumbleguts
hates noisy people, especially boys.
The only things that Mr. Grumbleguts
loves are his tomato plants.

Con (yelling) "I think I'm going to be smashed to smithereens!"

Crash! ... Smash!

Josh (peering over the fence) "Are you OK?"

Con "*Eeerrrrhh* I think I might be dead."

Josh "Well, you're talking, so you must be alive."

Josh peers over the fence. The spaceship has crashed and Con is lying in the middle of the wreckage.

Con "I think I must be really hurt!
I'm covered in blood."

Josh "That's not blood, they're
squashed tomatoes. Quick Con!
Mr. Grumbleguts is coming!"

Con springs to his feet and starts
to wipe off all the squashed tomatoes.
Mr. Grumbleguts comes running
towards them, shaking his head,
waving his hands and yelling.

Con "Oh no, what will we do now?"

Josh "Maybe we could help him make some tomato sauce—now that he's got all these squashed tomatoes."

Con "I don't think he's looking too interested in that just now. Quick, I've got to get back over the fence!"

Con (climbing over the fence) "I wish we had a real spaceship now. I think it might be a good time for a trip to another galaxy."

Con "I think that it's time we went to the park."

Josh "You're right, and the sooner the better."

aliens Creatures from outer space.
Aliens usually have one eye and green
snot running down their faces.

astronaut A person that has been
trained to travel into space.

blast-off! When the spaceship takes off
for its trip into space.

captain The person who is in charge of
the spaceship.

launch pad Where the spaceship gets
launched from.

spaceship The vehicle you use to travel
into space.

33

Space Must-dos

☞ Make sure that you ask permission before you start to make your spaceship from materials in your father's garage.

☞ Don't launch your spaceship from beside your neighbour's fence— especially if your neighbour is like Mr. Grumbleguts.

☞ If you ever see an alien, make sure that you give them a tissue. They're sure to have a runny nose.

☞ Always take a telescope with you if you go flying in a spaceship, so that you can look back at Earth.

☞ Take plenty of food with you. Flying a spaceship is sure to make you hungry.

☞ Make sure that you always wear a helmet, even if it's your bike helmet. You never know where you're going to land.

☞ Paint the word "Captain" on your helmet. It makes you look important.

☞ Wear a raincoat. If you get attacked by aliens, they might cover you with green snot!

Space Instant Info

 The first spaceship launched into space was *Sputnik 2*, which was launched from Russia in 1957. It orbited Earth with its passenger Laika, who was a dog.

 If you're thinking about being an astronaut, then you need to be really fit and healthy. You also need to be really good at maths and science.

 Neil Armstrong was the first man to walk on the Moon.

 When you fly into space you get into zero gravity, which means that you float around, sort of like a bird, but without wings.

The space suits that astronauts from NASA wear have twelve layers. It takes astronauts 45 minutes to put their suits on.

In 1965, a Russian woman called Valentina Tereshkova became the first woman to go into space.

The NASA-German solar probes *Helios 1* and *Helios 2* are the fastest spacecrafts. They reach speeds of 252,800 kilometres an hour during their orbits of the Sun.

BOYS RULE!
Think Tank

1 What is a launch pad?

2 What is an alien?

3 What is zero gravity?

4 Do countdowns go from 1 to 10, or from 10 to 1?

5 If your spaceship has orbited Earth, what has it done?

6 Who was the first man to walk on the Moon?

7 What does the "Man in the Moon" eat?

8 Is a spaceship faster than a car?

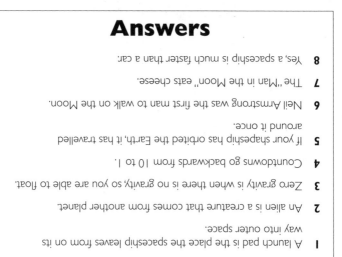

Answers

8 Yes, a spaceship is much faster than a car.

7 The "Man in the Moon" eats cheese.

6 Neil Armstrong was the first man to walk on the Moon.

5 If your shapeship has orbited the Earth, it has travelled around it once.

4 Countdowns go backwards from 10 to 1.

3 Zero gravity is when there is no gravity, so you are able to float.

2 An alien is a creature that comes from another planet.

1 A launch pad is the place the spaceship leaves from on its way into outer space.

How did you score?

- If you got all 8 answers correct, then you're ready to pilot your own spacecraft.

- If you got 6 answers correct, then you're ready for a trip into orbit, but only as the co-pilot!

- If you got fewer than 4 answers correct, then you're meant to stay on the ground—at least till you learn more about space travel.

Felice → ← Phil

Hi Guys!

We have heaps of fun reading and want you to, too. We both believe that being a good reader is really important and so cool.

Try out our suggestions to help you have fun as you read.

At school, why don't you use "Space Invaders" as a play and you and your friends can be the actors. Set the scene for your play. Bring some big boxes to school to make your spaceship. Use a smaller box for the space monitor. Make sure you're wearing your crash helmets before you blast-off.

So ... have you decided who is going to be Con and who is going to be Josh? Now, with your friends, read and act out our story in front of the class.

We have a lot of fun when we go to schools and read our stories. After we finish the children all clap really loudly. When you've finished your play your classmates will do the same. Just remember to look out the window—there might be a talent scout from a television channel watching you!

Reading at home is really important and a lot of fun as well.

Take our books home and get someone in your family to read them with you. Maybe they can take on a part in the story.

Remember, reading is fun.

So, as the frog in the local pond would say, Read-it!

And remember, Boys Rule!

Felice "Have you ever seen an alien?"

Phil "I think I have, but I'm not sure!"

Felice "What do mean, you're not sure?"

Phil "Well, I think I might have seen a group of aliens!"

Felice "Now that would be scary."

Phil "I heard all this strange noise coming from my sister's room."

Felice "What did you do?"

Phil "I walked into her room. It was aliens—girl aliens. There were six of them, and they were all talking at the same time."

Felice "Now that is 'alien'!"

What a Laugh!

Q What did the scientist say when the astronaut came back from the Moon with a bag of bones?

A Looks like the cow didn't jump over the Moon after all!

BOYS RULE!

Gone Fishing   The Tree House   Golf Legends   Camping Out   Bike Daredevils

 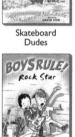   

Water Rats   Skateboard Dudes   Tennis Ace   Basketball Buddies   Secret Agent Heroes

Wet World   Rock Star   Pirate Attack   Olympic Champions   Race Car Dreamers

  Hit the Beach   Rotten School Day   Halloween Gotcha!   Battle of the Games   On the Farm

 44

BOYS RULE! books are available from most booksellers.
For mail order information please call Rising Stars
on 0870 40 20 40 8 or visit www.risingstars-uk.com